2-2-02
Warm Wishes
Kay Witschen ♡

W9-DHS-813

Kay dedicates this book to husband, Dick.

Norma dedicates this book to Rosanne, Bill and Carol.

i

CLINKER'S SHADOW

by

KAY WITSCHEN

Illustrated by
NORMA LUCKEMEYER

CLINKER'S SHADOW

Clinker did not like to see summer coming to an end. "I think it's time to take my trip around the countryside," he told his friends.

Some of the dogs that met in the neighborhood meadow every day laughed at Clinker.

"Why do you do that every year?" asked old Sparky.

"I like to visit new places before the snows come. And because

I want to see more of the World than the meadow." answered Clinker.

Jake the Husky spoke up. "What direction are you going?"

"I'm going in the direction of the sunset. I heard someone say that is West."

All the dogs nodded their heads in agreement. Clinker said his goodbyes and started off through the meadow.

"Clinker deserves a little relaxation after all the trouble he had with that flea in his ear this summer," said Tippee.

Clinker traveled to the center of the little town nearby as he

knew the man in the butcher shop always had a treat for him. As

he made his way to the back of the butcher shop he had the funniest

feeling that he was being followed.

He turned his head

VERY

SLOWLY

but saw nothing behind him and decided it must be his

imagination.

Clinker scratched at the back door of the butcher shop but when the door opened it was NOT his friend. It was a man he had never seen before.

SCAT!

BEAT IT!

GET LOST!

"Get out of here! I'm tired of all you hounds scratching at my door," he shouted.

Well **EX-CUSE** me, thought Clinker.

I know when I'm not wanted.

7

As Clinker traveled further out of town he could not get over the feeling that he was being followed. Looking back he caught a glimpse of something and decided to hide in the bushes and find out once and for all what was going on.

Clinker

WATCHED

and

WATCHED

and

WAITED

and

WAITED

8

At last the culprit came into view. A little kitten, walking ever so softly, was following the path that Clinker had taken.

Clinker jumped out from the bushes and shouted **"WHY ARE YOU FOLLOWING ME?** I don't want company and I especially don't want a **CAT** tagging along behind me."

"Oh, Clinker
I think you're swell
I just want
to be your pal"

"I do not **NEED** a pal. I just want you to leave me alone.

If you keep following me you may find out just how mean I can be.

Now scoot - go home - in other words

GET LOST!!!"

The kitten had a tiny tear in his eye but he sat still and

watched as Clinker took off running down the road.

By evening, Clinker was getting tired. When at last he came to an old barn he went inside and curled up on a pile of straw. He was soon fast asleep, dreaming happy dreams.

"**ACHOO! ACHOO!**" Clinker woke up to something tickling his nose. He could not believe his eyes when he saw the kitten curled up beside him.

"How did you catch up with me, you pest? And what's your name? How can I even yell at you if I don't know your name?"

*"I'm sorry to say
I have no name.
No friends, no food
No home to claim."*

"That's not my problem. One thing you're not going to be is my shadow. Now get out of here. Go back where you came from!"

Clinker traveled for weeks, visiting farms along the way. Old friends and new friends shared their food with him and made him welcome. He always left a little food behind but he told himself it was not because of that pesty kitten but because he was too full. He knew

12

the kitten was still back there somewhere and when it got too close he would yell, "Shadow, get away from me - and I mean it."

Shadow never answered, but kept on following Clinker as the days went by.

The weather was getting colder and colder and Clinker knew it was time to turn around and start home. He decided to take a shortcut across a lake that was covered with a thin layer of ice. He had done this before and knew that if he was careful it would be safe.

He was about halfway across the lake when he

heard a tiny voice calling "help, help."

He ran back toward the sound.

"Help me please
I've fallen through
I promise then
I won't follow you."

HELP!!

Oh I don't believe this. More trouble. This is scary - the ice is cracking everywhere underneath me.

Clinker crept toward the hole in the ice where Shadow was barely keeping his head above water as his paws were slipping further and further off the edge. "Hold on Shadow and let's hope our guardian angels are with us."

Clinker grabbed the fur on the back of Shadow's neck.

Once he got a good hold he inched his way backwards from the

hole to solid ground.

He brushed Shadow's fur as dry as he could and cuddled the

shivering kitten close to him to try and keep him from freezing to death.

By the next morning Shadow was looking much better.

"Clinker, thank you
For all you have done
Along with the angels
It seems we have won."

"O.K., O.K. Don't get all emotional on

me here. You can travel home with me

and from there on - you're on your own.

Just do me a favor and don't tell any of

my friends about this."

18

SHH!!!

"Boys and girls
I think you see
That Clinker really
does LOVE ME!"

THE END